steady diet of nothing

Also by Cynthia Cruz

POETRY

Back to the Woods

Hotel Oblivion

Guidebooks for the Dead

Dregs

How the End Begins

Wunderkammer

The Glimmering Room

Ruin

CULTURAL CRITICISM

The Melancholia of Class: A Manifesto for the Working Class

Disquieting: Essays on Silence

steady diet of nothing

A NOVEL

CYNTHIA CRUZ

FOUR WAY BOOKS
TRIBECA

LIBRARY OF CONGRESS CATALOGING-IN-PUBLICATION DATA
Names: Cruz, Cynthia, author.
Title: Steady diet of nothing / Cynthia Cruz.
Identifiers: LCCN 2023004472 (print) | LCCN 2023004473 (ebook) | ISBN
    9781954245662 (trade paperback) | ISBN 9781954245679 (ebook)
Subjects: LCGFT: Fiction.
Classification: LCC PS3603.R893 S74 2023 (print) | LCC PS3603.R893
    (ebook) | DDC 811/.6--dc23/eng/20230210
LC record available at https://lccn.loc.gov/2023004472
LC ebook record available at https://lccn.loc.gov/2023004473

This book is manufactured in the United States of America and printed on
acid-free paper.

Four Way Books is a not-for-profit literary press. We are grateful for the assistance
we receive from individual donors, public arts agencies, and private foundations
including the NEA, NEA Cares, Literary Arts Emergency Fund, and the
New York State Council on the Arts, a state agency.

NEW YORK STATE OF OPPORTUNITY. | **Council on the Arts**

PROUD MEMBER

[clmp]

We are a proud member of the Community of Literary Magazines and Presses.

Will we leave the last place burning?
Or do we just get leaving?
—Fugazi

steady diet of nothing

chapter one

Everywhere I went I brought Pinkie, my pink and white stuffed rabbit, with me. I knew people made fun of me, but I couldn't help myself. I couldn't go anywhere without her.

I was in Chinatown with my sister. She was on a secret mission so she left me on the street, leaning against a wall. After she had been gone for a while, a man walked up to me like he knew me. He was wearing a brown suit, carrying a briefcase.

"You and the rabbit," he said. "Twenty dollars."

I didn't say anything. I never do. I just stared at his face, his soft girl hands. I might have stopped breathing. I was afraid he was going to keep moving closer, that he would come close and touch me.

Luckily, my sister appeared out of nowhere.

She pushed him, threw her bag at him, and grabbed my hand. We ran down the narrow alley laughing hysterically. We kept running until we couldn't run anymore.

Around the corner at an all-night donut shop slash kiosk she bought us some donuts with pink and orange sprinkles. We bought packs of cigarettes and small paper cups of coffee. On the way out, I took a handful of penny candy. My favorites: pink and yellow Laffy Taffy and Halloween-sized Reese's Peanut Butter Cups. I hid them in my pockets, saving them for later.

We drove back down Highway One in my sister's red Karmann Ghia. The convertible top down, we smoked cigarette after cigarette, blasting the same song over and over all the way back down to Santa Cruz. Sometimes she'd steer too close to the edge and I knew for sure we were going over—

*

I showed up at the Blue House with Pinkie in one arm and a plastic bag with a bunch of my stuff in the other.

The night before a girl I didn't know walked up to me. She had long black hair and a short leather mini skirt.

I was standing outside the 7-11. She said her name was Darby. She came right up to me and touched my arm. "Are you a ghost?" she said. Then she grabbed me.

"Let's go, I'm taking you home."

But before she brought me to the Blue House she brought me to see Toby.

Toby was a skater. He had a buzz cut and dark eyes and his arms and neck were riddled in tattoos: words in gothic text and elaborate green, red and orange Chinese dragons, beautiful laces of ink ribboning up and down his arms. He was sitting outside a dilapidated building looking bored, smoking.

Darby said she wanted to give me something, that I had seemed so defeated standing there in the parking lot, a dazed look on my face. So, as farewell to my old life, she said, she asked Toby to give me a tattoo.

When me and Darby walked up, Toby nodded his head at Darby and reached out his hand. I found out later he was straight edge, that he had been clean for years. His face looked really serious and sad. He glanced at me, but he didn't smile.

He shook my hand and said, "My name's Toby, what's yours?"

"Candy," I said.

I looked at his hands. His nails were bitten down and he had one small blue tattoo on his index finger, an *x*. On his other hand, on one of his fingers, he was wearing a silver band with his name engraved on the inside of it, "Toby."

"Come on," he said.

Darby and I followed him into the building.

His makeshift studio was an abandoned warehouse he'd been using for cutting hair and tattoo work. But the police had been by a bunch of times and now there were warrants pasted on the doors of the building. Starting the next day they'd be locking everything up. So he'd packed two small cardboard boxes already, taped them shut. But he still had two chairs set out. I sat in one, he sat in the other and Darby left the room to smoke.

After Darby went outside, me and Toby sat across each from other for a long time in silence, smoking intermittently. I asked him where he was from. When he talked I could barely hear him. I had to lean in close. He was wearing a plain white t-shirt and black worker pants. He smelled sweet like candy mixed with cigarettes.

He talked slow. He told me he was from Virginia, that he left because there was nothing there for him. But also, he said, he had to get away from his family. He didn't explain, but I knew. I knew as soon as he started talking, that we'd come from the same place. I could see it in the way he held his body, the way he had to fight to get the words out. He didn't have to say anything else.

I nodded my head, *Yes.*

He told me he wanted to draw a small blue star inside my right arm. He walked away to get some ink and then he came back up to me, took my arm, and drew a star on my skin with his finger.

I shook my head, *No.*

He gave me a tiny slip of paper and I quickly drew an image of a painting I once saw on the front of an album of a girl warrior in the apocalypse, holding a machine gun.

Toby looked at my picture. Then he looked at me. He didn't say anything.

It took five hours and by the middle of it, my arm was throbbing. It was bruised and red.

Toby suggested we finish the rest of the work the next day. But I really wanted to get it done. You never know what's going to happen. People vanish, they disappear and they never come back. I didn't know what was going to happen to me, where I was going, or if I would ever see Toby again. Plus, I wanted that picture of the girl on my arm.

I made him fill in all the colors, the blue in her t-shirt, the red in her running shorts, the bright yellow of her hair. It took forever and it hurt so bad I could taste the pain in my mouth. When he was done, the tattoo took up my entire arm.

Toby rubbed a cotton ball with cream on the tattoo and bandaged my arm up with plastic wrap.

"Welcome home," he said.

*

We stayed that night in Toby's studio. Darby was up until the morning sitting in one of Toby's swivel chairs she'd wheeled outside the door, drinking beer, smoking and listening to music on her earphones.

Toby kept trying to take care of me: offering me food, cigarettes, more cream for my arm.

But I just sat in the dark, not talking, staring off. It wasn't that I didn't want to talk, it's just that I couldn't.

The next morning before we left, Toby cut my hair. It was my idea. I told him I wanted to cut it all off, start over. I knew that's what he did, that's what they all did. They shaved their heads and then when it started to grow out, they shaved it again. It was a form of unstated ritual. A form of communal discipline. I knew it from my brother and his friends. I wanted to be a part of that.

My hair wasn't really long but it was long enough: to my ears. I'd had it like that since I started high school. Bleached, it looked like a wig. But I didn't want that anymore.

Toby didn't want to do it and he said so. But I kept asking until, finally, he gave in. By the time he was finished, though my hair wasn't buzzed, it was short like a boy's.

In the morning, after Toby cut my hair, I thanked him. Then, I just stood there, looking at his face, then looking at my hands.

Aside from the two boxes he'd packed, he was leaving everything else behind. He told me and Darby he was going away for a while. When I asked where, he wouldn't say.

As he was talking, I kept looking at his hands, he kept touching one hand to the other, nervously; playing with his ring, taking it off, sliding it back on his finger.

I wanted to say it, but I couldn't: I was hoping I would get to see him again.

When Darby first brought me to the Blue House I was scared. I didn't know what to expect.

The House was stucco and painted pale blue. Inside, there was graffiti on the walls and stools and couches that had been dragged in, some old rugs, and milk crates. In the main room, against the wall, there was a bookshelf filled with books and on one low shelf, a record player and piles of records. Throughout the House there were ashtrays, and more stacks of books and records. The story was that the House had been abandoned and now it belonged to the state but the state didn't want it. There was no glass in the windows, just cardboard duct-taped where the windows should have been. The floors were concrete and at night we slept in a heap of blankets.

Germ's real name was Jeremy. He put his hand out and shook mine, smiling. He was tall and lanky with big dark eyes. Like all the boys at the Blue House, his head was shaved and he was wearing a t-shirt and worker pants, boots. He had tattoos on his arms. He was from LA, the child of some famous actress. He ran away from home when he was fifteen when his stepdad started coming into his bedroom at night, drunk. He said he'd been living on the streets in Hollywood until things got out of hand, his voice trailing off.

Napalm was the only boy who didn't have his head shaved. He had long reddish-blonde curly hair and a face full of freckles. I couldn't understand him. When he was talking to me, he talked so fast. But it was alright. Something about the air quality and danger. After he gave me a hug he ran off and I didn't see him again.

Tiger was tall like Germ with really short bleached-blonde hair and black eyebrows and a really pretty face, like a girl's. He was smiling when he saw me.

"Welcome," he said. "I've seen you around."

When I asked, he wouldn't tell me what he meant.

He had a beer in one hand and a cigarette in the other. We were outside now, on the steps and he was asking me questions about where I came from and how I found out about the House. I told him my sister told me, that she was living here, too. When I told him who my sister was he smiled and looked away.

Someone had turned the music on in the back room and it was blasting into the front now.

When I turned to Tiger to ask him what he knew about my sister, he was gone.

That night I met Talia and Scooter, two girls also from LA. They'd been living at the House for over a year. They kept looking at each other and laughing while I was talking, like they had their own private language. Talia had long blonde hair and was wearing black jeans and a Bambi t-shirt and black boots; red lipstick. Scooter had short, dyed black hair. It was slicked back like a man's and she was wearing a button-up shirt tucked into a black pair of men's slacks. She kept looking at me and laughing. After a while I walked away to find Darby for a smoke.

I found her in the front room, sitting alone in a green La-Z-Boy chair. Her eyes were closed and she was listening to music on her earphones. When I tapped her on the shoulder, her eyes opened quickly and she took her earphones off.

"Come on, let's go," she said, taking my hand.

She dragged me outside to the front steps where she pulled a bottle of peach schnapps and a pack of Marlboro Reds from her leather jacket.

"Welcome home, Candy," she said, giving me a hug.

When I first started hanging out at the Blue House I could tell the other girls didn't like me. I knew when I met Talia and Scooter that there was something about me they didn't like. But no one ever said anything so it was hard to tell.

I never wore make-up and when I showed up I had cut all my hair off. I think they thought I was full of myself because I never talked, that they thought I was better than everyone else. When I'd walk into a room, they would stop what they were doing and wouldn't start up again until I'd left the room. And it didn't help that I mostly only hung out with the boys.

I found out later there were rumors at the House about me: that they thought I'd come from a rich family in Marin, and that I wore my dead brother's clothes.

No one knew Napalm's real name or where he came from.

He wore fatigues, combat boots and an orange fluorescent armband.

"For the coming Armageddon," he'd say.

Sometimes he wore plastic desert goggles, the kind the military wear.

He'd build paper bombs, beautiful bombs, red, like Chinese paper lanterns. He made them with paper, powder, batteries and flame. Love bombs, word bombs, he blew things up just to watch them explode.

He had big hair—wild, like an animal. He'd sit on the front steps of the Blue House talking to himself or to anyone who would stop and listen. Like a soldier in his washed-out fatigues and a bag of his fire stuff, he'd sit outside the Blue House to keep all of us safe.

He made this gigantic box, this thing he called The Shed, out of old wood and metal. Inside were stacks and stacks of old books and manuals: classics and the Bible, military handbooks and How-to-Bomb books. Gas masks and breathing tubes, flak jackets and mace, everything in piles.

He had notebooks in the Shed: on Hiroshima, Nagasaki, the Nevada test site, the carpet bombings in Dresden and Cambodia, depleted uranium. And he had notebooks on what to do when the end comes. Saline treatment for chemical burns, things to mix up for nuclear sickness, nerve agents, what to do—he had it all figured out.

His notebooks were so thick, they wouldn't close: he had so much stuff crammed in there. Xeroxed copies of what to look for: in the eyes, on the skin, in the behavior of animals. Before things go crazy and then for afterwards. It was like a secret library and he wouldn't let anyone near it.

While all of us were inside the Blue House drinking, smoking and laughing, Napalm was outside, busy preparing for the end of the world.

There were rumors that Napalm had been living on the streets since he was ten. That his dad died of a heroin overdose when he was a baby and that his mom was a junkie and prostitute, that she lived on the streets in Portland.

Under highway overpasses, in buildings long abandoned for asbestos or rat infestations, Napalm cooked up his own MREs on his homemade foil-and-coat-hanger grill.

Napalm would go on these rants and he couldn't come back down. Reading more and more, listening to secret frequencies on his broken radio, taking notes.

Knowing what he knew messed with his mind, made him more paranoid. Nicaragua, Guatemala, Afghanistan, the Chicago School of Economics and the US coup in Chile. He told me about Camp Perry, "The Farm," and the experimental torture techniques the US used. LSD, he said, waterboarding, he explained. I nodded, as if I knew, not wanting to interfere with his lesson.

We'd find him one morning, downtown, blowing things up or ranting madly on top of a plastic crate. Then the police would come and cart him off to another psych ward.

"You'd better be ready," he'd say, frantically, his hair pulled back in a woman's scarf.

I'm like him, too. When I was little all I did was read books. My mother would drop me off at the public library and leave me there all day. She wouldn't come get me until nighttime. So I escaped into books and pretty soon it's all I did.

I read about world history, and about the wars, the CIA and the US military. And the more I knew, the more paranoid I became, knowing how the systems and structures underneath everything make all of us sick.

The more you know, the closer you veer to the edge. It makes you crazy. And if you're crazy, you can't do anything.

Darby told me Toby dropped out of school. That it was too hard to stay. Not the schoolwork but being followed around all day by the other kids, calling him names. One day he just up and left. And it wasn't any better at home. With his dad working all day in the chemical factory and his mom at home passed out from drinking. Saying things to him that didn't make any sense.

He'd spend his days out in the skatepark riding the fury out of his body. He'd end up injured: bruises and sprains. Sometimes he'd come home in the middle of the night and nobody would notice he'd ever even been gone. Sometimes he'd just stay out all night instead, sleeping on park benches, living on cola and donuts.

I hadn't seen him since he gave me my tattoo and I was worried about him.

I imagined him, quiet, someplace. Cold, faraway. And I sent him private messages through my mind.

Toby, you're going to be okay, I'd tell him.

Toby, I am going to see you, soon.

Toby had burn marks on his arms and when I asked him he would never tell me why. And small white lightning scars on his face you could see only if you got real close.

When he was sleeping, I'd lean over him, carefully, and watch his face as he was dreaming.

When he talked he talked in broken utterances, in fragments. He'd hesitate before speaking, stopping himself after he'd begun. And though I couldn't always decipher exactly what he was saying, I understood. We were both formed by the same elements. I knew the world he came from, the ways the world had altered him. He didn't have to say anything. I knew.

When Darby was little, the state came and took her from her sisters. She said the neighbors called Child Protection and they came that same day. Each of the girls was separated, each sent to a different foster home hell.

The first home Darby was sent to was a mobile home in the desert where she babysat her foster sisters and brothers, watching them while the foster mom had sex with the neighbor. Each foster home she was sent to was worse than the one before.

When Darby arrived at the Blue House she had bruises on her body and her face. She was wearing a long blonde wig with horse bangs, a black leather mini skirt, and these really tall black leather boots. She looked like a hologram or a cut-out from a fairy tale.

Darby said she woke up in the middle of the night one time and her mother wasn't in the house. So she and her sisters went looking for her.

They found her outside in her nightgown, wandering through the weeds. She had a flashlight in her hand and she was calling out their names.

Darby had brown hair and huge dark eyes. Her father, who she'd never met, was Mexican. She grew up with her mom outside Reno in Sparks, Nevada.

Her mom was a waitress at one of the truck stops so Darby and her sisters grew up in a red leather booth in the diner where her mom worked. She'd tell us about all these characters she'd grown up with. The other waitresses, of course, who would sometimes take turns taking care of Darby and her sisters when her mom stayed out late. But also sometimes she'd talk about the men—the way she described them was like they were ghosts—appearing out of nowhere and then vanishing again. All the men—the different men—becoming one. She never got into it—she'd stop talking when it got too close. Whatever it was, it was gone now, a memory she'd pushed down into her unconscious a million years ago.

She carried these small black and red pocketknives with her and she always wore the same black leather jacket. And she cursed like a man, which was funny, because she was so small, her body so tiny, as she acted so tough. I think it was a form of self-protection. But inside she was just a little kid, like all of us.

Darby and her sisters and her mom had been living inside a car garage her mother was renting. With no heat or electricity. They all slept in a mess of blankets and sleeping bags on the floor in a pile: all three girls in two Star Wars sleeping bags.

Then one day the case worker came in on an unannounced visit. Saw the way they were living and took the girls away.

That was when Darby was little, and she hadn't seen her mom or her sisters since.

In the Blue House there were beer bottles stashed around. If you wanted one you just took one. Same thing with cigarettes, you'd just ask and there were always extra packs lying around. When we were hungry, someone always had something to eat or money. We never went without. Even clothes, when I went to the House, I only had what I was wearing but then everyone gave me something. Talia gave me a pair of black boots, Tiger gave me his pale blue satin bomber, and Darby gave me some of her t-shirts and sweatshirts. We also took stuff from stores when we needed to.

The House was like any other house except that it was abandoned and emptied out. And, of course, there was no electricity. We girls hung out on the stools and old chairs in the front room. The boys stayed mostly in the back where music was always playing. It was Guy, Germ, Tiger, and Napalm. And then Toby who reappeared suddenly after three months out of nowhere.

One day there was a knock on the door and someone went to get it and the next thing I knew Toby appeared. He had nothing with him, nothing but his skateboard. I saw him as he was walking through the corridor—he was too thin and he looked sad. But I was so happy to see him again I just ran up to him.

Later, when we were alone, he gave me his ring. I told him no, that he should keep it, that I didn't deserve it. But he insisted, he put the ring on a silver chain necklace then he put the chain around my neck, shutting the tiny clasp in the back. "It's yours," he said. "Take good care of it."

His giving me his ring made me sad though it should have made me happy. It seemed like he was giving his ring to me as an act of saying goodbye. I kept telling myself that it wasn't true. But I couldn't make myself believe it.

The boys in the Blue House were older than us: seventeen and eighteen and most of them had started to dabble in heroin. No one ever said anything about it. But we all knew. And even though they were older than us and boys, I was never afraid of them. They seemed like older brothers to me—they tried to take care of us, and of each other. It makes sense—we'd all escaped near death and now we had finally found a home. Of course we would risk our lives for each other. We had no one else.

We girls smoked cigarettes and drank beer in the front room or out on the steps. Hard drugs were out of the question. We panhandled downtown at the bus station to make enough money to pay for cigarettes and beer, telling tourists our car was out of gas, that we needed money to drive back home to Los Gatos.

The tourists would always give us money. We still looked okay—so they believed us, that we were stranded suburban teenagers.

I was still young and I looked it: child-like, with my full cheeks and baby fat. Soon though my face would become angled like the boys', my thin arms covered in scars.

chapter two

We spent our afternoons hustling for money downtown to buy alcohol. Then, once we'd collected enough, we'd make our way to the Liquor Barn. Two juvenile delinquents: Darby in her long blonde wig, her leather mini skirt, her tall black boots; me in my jeans and t-shirt, my blonde hair cut short. And always pretty soon some older dude would come up, ask us what we were up to, what our names were, pretending to be interested. They'd take our money, a handful of singles and coins, vanish into the store and race right back with whatever we'd asked for. Then they'd stand around for a while waiting for us to offer them favors.

We always asked for vodka or schnapps. Whatever would get us drunkest the fastest. And there was always an endless supply of dudes on the make we could charm into buying us booze. And we knew what they were thinking: that for buying us alcohol, they'd be getting some sweet favor. We knew about the transaction: what they wanted in return, even though it was never spoken. They were not buying us booze for nothing. We knew that.

We'd be standing, me and Darby in silence, just wishing the dude would disappear, he'd be making small talk with us as if we were adults, as if we were his equals. We'd stand around for a while, me looking at Darby, Darby looking at me, rolling our eyes, winking at each other, until we just couldn't take it anymore. One of us would grab the brown bag from him and we'd sprint, running as fast as we could out of the parking lot, down the street and away from there.

Napalm read about the effects of nerve agent: drool, dimmed and blurred vision, mass hysteria.

He'd tell us soon they wouldn't need to use drugs to fuck us up, that PSYOP were cheaper and easier to administer.

"It's everywhere," he'd tell us. "It seeps into your thoughts, takes over, until there's nothing left."

He pointed to magazines and newspapers, movies and television shows, saying that by the time you figure out what's happening, it's already taken root deep inside you.

"It used to be they used these weapons on the enemy," he'd explain. "But now we're the enemy."

"Football arenas," he'd say. "Mass conformism," his face contorted, changed with rage.

He'd read all these books: the German philosophers, the French theorists: "Adorno," he'd say, "Marcuse." "Deleuze and Guattari." Half the time no one knew what he was talking about. He'd barge into the room, an opened book in his hand, ready to begin one of his impromptu lectures.

We'd see him pacing outside in front of the House. We'd watch him diminishing as the hours passed until, in the end, he'd be sitting alone on the steps, shaking his head, looking like he might cry.

"No escape," he'd whisper now, talking to no one.

Napalm had these stashes of emergency supplies: iodine pills and anti-radiation pills, K1 and K103 pills stocked-up for when the fallout happens. Said he had enough for all of us.

And meals: kits, he called them, military rations. He said he got them from this guy downtown and whenever he saw me he was always trying to give me one.

Handing me a brown bag packed with a foil-wrapped meal, he'd say, "You need to eat, Candy. It's fucked up, what you're doing."

I'd look away, trying to avoid his gaze.

"You know you're going to die, if you keep that shit up," he'd sneer.

I don't know how he knew, but he did. He didn't baby me about it, either. He didn't have any patience for it. He could see that what I was doing had something to do with death and, obviously, he had no tolerance for that. He spent all his time trying to figure out how to keep us alive and here I was slowly decimating my body.

He'd watch me when everyone else was eating and I was just sitting there, pushing my food around, pretending to eat. He'd stare at me until my face felt hot.

"Candy," he'd say, like a grandmother. "Candy, I see you."

It was this big mansion up in the hills near the university. A huge Victorian that looked like a dollhouse but blown-up in size, and an enormous yard out front with these gigantic billowing trees. There were all these cars parked out front in the U-shaped driveway: Audis and Volvos, a few Mercedes. We weren't deterred, though. We walked right up to the front door like the house was our own.

The front doors were beveled glass and there was a note at the door that said, "Push." So we did.

The dining room was buzzing with all these hipster college kids drinking champagne in fancy glasses. A real cocktail party: girls in dresses standing in small circles, giggling.

All week there had been a flyer pasted downtown on the telephone poles announcing the party. It said on the flyers that there would be free food and booze so we figured we'd show up. We thought it was strange to put up flyers for a party but that didn't stop us.

When we walked into the room everyone froze, became statues. It was pretty obvious that, though it was an "open" party, that apparently anyone could attend, we weren't the target audience the flyer had meant to be addressing.

As soon as we walked in, the girl throwing the party walked up to us, she was wearing a pink and white polka dot halter dress, heels, her fingernails painted pale pink. Her hands were shaking and she said, "Girls, you should probably go."

All of us laughed: she called us "*Girls*."

They were obviously the sons and daughters of the university deans or doctors. Kids from families with money who had been to private school, who would be going off to Ivy League colleges, Berkeley or Stanford, would become art historians or curators. They had put the flyers up downtown to bring in the underground culture, punk rock, the real thing. They had thought they wanted to experience something "cutting edge," something "real," but now here we were and they wanted nothing to do with us.

"But we just got here," Darby whined.

She was looking around, like me, trying to see if there was anything worth taking.

I was frozen, staring at the chandeliers, the pretty soft rugs with tiny caravanning elephants. Toby was behind me. I could feel his breath on my neck. "Candy," he whispered. I grabbed his hand and led him up the stairs to find an empty bedroom. After four rooms, I stopped counting. When I opened the door of what appeared to be the fifth, I dragged him inside and we shut the door behind us.

The room was painted mint-green and the curtains were shut. There was a giant bed in the middle of the room, a chandelier, a fireplace and, in the corner, a tiny library of books. I walked to the books, pulled one out. It was a giant hardcopy of Dostoyevsky's *Crime and Punishment*. I shoved the book in my bag. Then I walked over to the bed and lay down.

We knew we had to leave soon, that we couldn't stay in the room, not for more than a few minutes, so we didn't bother talking.

Right then there was a knock on the door, and then Darby's voice, "Come on, let's go."

I grabbed Toby's hand and we walked out of the room. We went back down the spiral staircase into the kitchen where Darby was standing.

Toby and I walked into the kitchen and over to the refrigerator. We stood there for a while. I was staring at all the tiny, wrapped servings of food as Toby was taking as many beers as he could.

"Come on, help me," he said. When I heard his voice, I snapped out of it.

As me and Toby were packing the beers into a bag, Darby came and stood next to me, standing in the cold light of the refrigerator.

"What the hell."

She was staring at the tiny, pretty, pink, lime-green and yellow displays of food. Some kind of desserts that had apparently been catered for the event.

"Come on," I said, grabbing Darby by the hand. "We have to go."

I knew they had probably already called the cops on us. And when they arrived, they'd be taking us all back to juvenile hall. Or worse. We couldn't risk it, we had to get out of there.

As we were making our way through the mansion toward the front door, I heard someone yell, "Come on, let's go!" By then we had all started running.

But I stopped for a moment when I saw a giant brown and white teddy bear on a shelf above one of the fireplaces.

"I have to have that."

And I grabbed it. And it was really big—so I was running with this giant bear in my arms, and laughing. When I got outside, everyone was running from the house out into the street. I saw Toby standing on the lawn, waiting for me. I ran right into him, the bear sandwiched between us. I couldn't stop laughing.

"His name is Toby," I said.

He grabbed the bear, took my hand, and we ran laughing all the way down the street, down the hill and back into the safety of the city.

Napalm was always thinking of America. I think he even dreamed about it: the Vets, how they'd come home from the wars, broken. He was always talking about what we do in the wars, how we kill civilians: mothers and children. Dropping our bombs on their hospitals, their orphanages.

He carried around these photographs he'd torn out from magazines and newspapers: of children on gurneys, their limbs missing, their small faces frozen in terror. He'd try giving them out to strangers downtown, handing out these tiny xeroxed photos of orphans, but no one would take them and then, always, the cops would come.

One night when everyone was inside the House drinking and listening to music, I just couldn't take it anymore. Toby had disappeared again and being in the House without him, having to listen to everyone laughing, having fun, it was just too much. Toby's absence was like a ghost. Toby's absence was a ghost. His absence was a presence.

I went outside to be alone. Napalm was sitting on the porch. When I opened the front door and saw him and said hello, he shook his head, looked away.

After a while, he started telling me about a man he saw on the television with half his face blown off. He said no matter what he did, he couldn't get the image out of his mind, like a series of x-rays that kept repeating in his head, building into one endless flow of memory.

I didn't see him again for a week or two. No one knew where he went. All of us worried he'd ended up back in the psych ward.

Napalm and Toby were always on my case saying I should eat. I had told Toby about my eating dilemma and he'd listened when I told him about why and when it began and why I was so scared to eat. Ever since then, he'd joined Napalm in his vigilance—

Even though I didn't want to, I'd eat for them. Because what I hate, more than anything, is making people worry about me. So I'd eat what they gave me.

Sometimes Toby would bring me my favorite: Laffy Taffy or soft caramels. He'd reach down into his pockets and pull out these handfuls of candy, dropping them in front of me in small piles.

"Here you go, hamster," he'd say, grinning.

I don't know where he got all that candy from. He probably stole it.

I didn't care. We'd eat the candy together, quickly, like starving children. Reading each other the stupid jokes on the back of the taffy wrappers, laughing for no good reason.

When Toby laughed something in him was altered. You could see the kid he once was. For that one moment in time, that tiny molecule of space, while we were laughing together, we were free.

One night we all went wheat pasting downtown. Talia, Scooter, Toby, Darby, Napalm and me. We'd made these posters, they said: *Steady Diet of Nothing*. It was from a Fugazi album. Under the words we pasted a picture of a girl's face that Napalm had been carrying around, a little girl living in poverty, her hands and face covered in dirt.

Scooter and Talia brought along some spray paint for the bridges and alleys. And Napalm had concocted a paste from who knows what. At one point, a cop car drove by real slow as we were working on one of the posters so we had to disperse. But as soon as the car vanished, we ran right back and finished pasting twenty more posters. We spray-painted every bridge we crossed that night and they never caught us, never even seemed to notice.

When we were done we ended up at the second bridge downtown, all of us having a middle-of-the-night picnic of peach schnapps and cigarettes on the side of the river. Sometime after that Germ and Guy vanished and then Talia, Scooter and Darby took off for the Boardwalk. Me and Toby walked over to the forest, this area behind the liquor store where the trees hadn't been cut down yet. We walked around a little and then when we found a bench we both sat down. I took out my cigarettes and offered one to Toby. I was hoping he'd tell me where he'd gone, why he kept disappearing. But he just sat there, his arms wrapped around his knees, silently staring off into space.

He looked different than when we first met, the night he gave me my tattoo. He had always been a skater punk, and hard-edge, but lately he'd lost what seemed like a mysterious amount of weight. I thought maybe he'd had a relapse, that maybe he'd been getting into something darker. He'd been getting into heroin like the rest of the boys.

I could tell he had something he wanted to tell me. He had this desperate look on his face.

"What's wrong?" I asked.

He shrugged and looked away.

Then he looked back at me and shook his head.

It was weird because Toby had been living on the streets for so long, I had always assumed he was tougher than the rest of us. But sitting there, in the dark, with him looking so tiny, he looked smaller than me, like a child. And for the first time, it occurred to me that maybe he didn't know. Maybe he was just as lost as I was.

I got up and walked over to him and hugged him. And he actually hugged me back. We stayed like that awhile: with our arms around each other, saying nothing. Time seemed not to be a factor. I don't know if we stayed like that for five minutes or an hour. Nothing mattered. Nothing mattered but what was happening to us. At a certain point I thought he maybe started to cry, silently, the way I do. But I couldn't be sure and I wasn't about to ask.

Finally, he stepped back and looked at me for a long time. He took my hand and we walked out of the forest back out into the noise of the city.

"Who is he? Who is your friend?" the girl asked.

She was looking at Toby. Her eyes were wrong.

"Wow, you're tall," she murmured.

I hadn't noticed there was anything wrong with her until she started talking. Her voice was rough like a boy's and she was talking too slow.

She was wearing what looked like kid's clothes: a dress with pink knee highs and white high-top sneakers with unicorns on them. You could tell by her face that she was older. She must have been nineteen, but she looked twelve.

"That's a nice bracelet," she said pointing to my Medic Alert bracelet. "Where'd you get it?"

The girl kept talking but we had already started walking away. I could hear her murmuring to herself, "Nothing, nothing."

After we walked a few blocks Toby told me he knew the girl, that she used to come by the Blue House. He said he'd forgotten her name but she used to be really smart.

I could tell there was something he wasn't telling me. I could see it in his face.

He looked sad. I had a feeling it had something to do with her maybe having been his girlfriend. And I didn't want to know. So I didn't ask him anything else.

Darby and I saw the cops take Napalm away, again.

He was downtown talking a mile a minute: Chernobyl, nuclear waste, the fallout desert. He had all these photographs with him of children with limbs missing.

Then pretty soon the cops arrived. Napalm was standing on a cart, talking too loud, his voice wavering, about to break. The photographs had fallen out of his hands and were now in a circle on the ground around him.

By the time Darby and I made our way over to where he was standing, the cops had already pushed him to the ground and cuffed him.

We ran up to the cops. Darby was telling them all this stuff about how Napalm was epileptic, how he had Tourette's, and that they had better be careful. But the cops weren't buying any of it. They dragged him away.

There was another cop sitting in a cop car. He was in the front seat eating french fries. We ran up to the car with Napalm in it and tried to get him free but the cop jumped out of the car, grabbed me by my arm and pushed me down.

By the time I got up the cops were already driving away with Napalm locked in the back seat.

I watched Napalm's round face staring at me from the back window as the car vanished, looking at me as if he had never seen me before.

Me and Toby were downtown. We had just bought all these albums at the record store. We were sitting on the curb, smoking, when a man walked up to us. He was really good-looking. He was tall and thin, he had black hair and was wearing an old gray suit. He looked like Nick Cave.

"You," he said, pointing to Toby. "You're beautiful."

I didn't know what to think. I thought for sure Toby would be mad, that he'd say something back to the man to make sure that he left, that he never came back, to let him know what he was saying, what he was doing, that it wasn't okay. But Toby just sat there, looking at the man, then looking at his hands, then looking away.

The man stood there for a while, staring at Toby. It was like he didn't see me, I didn't exist. When neither me or Toby said anything, the man lit a cigarette, looked at Toby and said, almost in a whisper, "Come on, come with me."

Toby looked confused like he didn't know whether he should stay or go.

Eventually the man left but not without walking right up to Toby, pulling out a fancy pen and scrap of paper, writing out his telephone number and then, touching Toby's arm, and handing him the slip of paper with his number written on it.

"Call me," he said, folding the tiny slip of paper in half. "Call me anytime."

After the man left I felt like crying. I wanted to say something but I didn't know what. Toby didn't say anything either. We both just sat there in the dark in silence, smoking.

I finally got up and walked away. I couldn't stop my mind from racing. It was trying to make sense of what had happened, but it couldn't.

I knew I had to do something to make it stop. I couldn't live another minute with the thoughts that were flooding my mind.

I wanted to go downtown and try to find the girl we had run into, the one I thought was Toby's ex. Maybe she could help. Stop the racing thoughts in my head. I had to get out of my body.

My mind was telling me, *Toby is gone.*

It was true, he was here, with me on the curb. But what was here with me was just his body. His mind, his spirit, was gone someplace else. And that place was where he was heading. Or he was there already. It didn't matter what I said or did. I needed to find someone to help me shut my mind down.

But after I got up to walk away, Toby came walking after me and we eventually made our way to this bar where they never check IDs. We stayed there all night, both of us drinking too much, until we were both really fucked up. At a certain point, he disappeared, I don't know where. I was getting free drinks from these guys who kept calling me Daisy.

"Daisy, you're so pretty," the one kept saying. "Daisy, why don't you come for a walk with me?" I knew it was dangerous, it always is. It's a tricky science, getting drunk without getting myself killed.

After a while, Toby reappeared. He was standing with this man who had his hand on his shoulder. I walked up, took the man's hand off, grabbed Toby's hand and led him out of the bar. I didn't ask—I never do—where he had been, or what he had been made to do. You could see it on his face.

"Come on," I said.

I have no idea how we made it back to the House. There are huge swaths of time I lost—thoughts and memories I will never get back.

When I woke the next morning, Toby was sleeping next to me, his hand in my hand.

chapter three

The street was a dead end with two factories on it: a recycling plant and a cannery. Abandoned cars were parked across from the factories. A metal gate separated the water from the end of the street. Someone had cut a hole in the gate in the exact shape of a human body.

Along the shore, adjacent to the dilapidated loading dock, a black tarp was laid out along the rocks. Near the tarp, huge plastic containers were stacked, filled with newspapers, magazines and books bleached from the sun.

Planks rose from the river, worn and swollen from years of water. Three cormorants stood on the stilts of the planks. Black oil-coated feathers made their wings and bodies appear wet. From below the depths, one bird appeared, its strange black body, slick and glistening, prehistoric, part bird, part fish, disappearing into the sky. After some time, it reappeared, diving back down into the water.

Napalm had reappeared mysteriously and when he did he began compulsively building these little houses for the feral cats. He built them from plastic buckets, cut holes in the front for them to enter. And he put old newspaper in each of the boxes to make small cat-sized beds. Big ones and little ones, he stacked them, one on top of the other. Eleven boxes, one for each of the cats to sleep in.

Medical bills in bags by the water's edge. One more person in
debt from illness. One more person whose home had been taken.
Newspaper and magazines worn from weather.

Old, frayed beach chairs, plastic crates, bags filled with clothing.
A huge pink plastic bowl filled with water for the cats, another of
Napalm's projects.

An old radio connected by wire to a shopping cart, the cart loaded
down with junk: books and magazines, stuffed animals, clothes, shoes,
empty bottles and cans in large plastic bags.

Me and Toby staggered out from the Blue House past the liquor store and up to the trees at the levee, what we called the Swamp.

Trashed La-Z-Boys floating in the sewage along with old 40-ounce bottles, kids' toys and pillows. Someone's radio was blaring a loud, indecipherable music.

Napalm was there already. He was sitting with Talia on a lime-green couch at the edge of the water, laughing.

Toby wrapped me in a medical blanket and then he dropped off to sleep.

I watched him as he slept, kissed his cold hands and his fingers.

How to build a cheap and simple survival still that will produce drinking water in a dry desert. Basic materials for setting this up are:

6-foot square sheet of clean plastic

2–4 quart capacity container

5-foot piece of flexible plastic tubing

Pick an unshaded spot for the still and dig a hole.
If no shovel is available, use a stick or your own hands.

I tugged at Toby's hand and whispered, "Look."

His eyes followed my hand which was pointing away from the edge of the bridge, over the water to a wading bird. As soon as he saw the white animal, he laughed.

Under the bridge was a Snowy Egret, an avian angel, its white body, perfect. Saturn-like rings, remnants from years of gas spills, trailed out from its tail, its thin legs. The bird stood knee-deep in the river, its head darting back and forth.

I watched Toby, how his smile changed the entire architecture of his face. Always sad, I never saw his face light-up like it did upon discovery. I'd made a habit of pointing out animals as soon as I'd see them. Feral cats and kittens were our favorites. But on the rare occasions when I'd spotted a mouse or raccoon, it was bliss watching his face.

"He looks like you," Toby said.

I leaned against his tall thin body, the two of us up against the railing of the bridge, staring at the beautiful alien creature.

I spent the weekend with Toby. Sometimes when we went out he'd wear a skinny tie or a tiny suit jacket. That's what he wore that weekend with his old black boots.

No one knew much about him. He told me he was from Virginia, that his dad and his granddads all worked in the factory in town. He was supposed to, too, but then he left. His mother drank all day. He'd come home and find her passed out on the living room couch or, if she wasn't passed out yet, saying things that made no sense. Garbled, confused. And sometimes, he said, she seemed really scared and that scared him, too. Especially when he was little. She'd call the hospital, ask the ambulance to come and get her. He'd ride with her all the way into town as she told him over and over how much she loved him. "I love you, you know that," she'd say. But the more she said it, the less he believed her. Eventually nothing had any meaning. His mother, his father gone all day, every day, working and still unable to take care of them. He eventually dropped out of high school. He and his brother started a band so that helped. But then his brother got into heroin and the band fell apart.

He left one morning with his skateboard and a hundred dollars. His brother had told him to come to Santa Cruz. It took him two weeks to make his way. He never told me how he got here, what happened. He just told me it was worth it because he met me.

1. Heroic stage
2. Honeymoon phase ("We got through it")
3. Disillusionment. Magnitude of loss.
4. The New Normal

I thought Toby was dying. I stayed awake all night watching his mouth. Making sure he didn't stop breathing. There were moments when his lips didn't seem to move and I couldn't hear his breath. His face was still so I'd say his name, "Toby," to make sure. He'd open his eyes, look at me, then fall back asleep. He never asked why I was saying his name. Maybe when he woke he didn't know why, couldn't remember. Maybe he thought I was part of the dream.

One night all of us drove up Highway One to San Francisco, the two-lane highway that jags along the Pacific coast, at the edge of the cliffs, one wrong turn and you'd crash into the ocean. We took turns driving, each one forcing the car to go a little faster until I was sure we were going to go over the edge. I was holding onto my rabbit, Pinkie, and smoking, laughing hysterically while I was crying.

Once we got to San Francisco, we didn't know what to do. But sure enough, Darby had a plan. She dragged us all up Polk Street. She said she knew some guy, or she used to know some guy, and she vaguely remembered where he lived. After about an hour of knocking on doors we finally found him.

And he was a disaster. All bones, his eyes sunken in. He looked like he hadn't eaten for years. He led us upstairs to his apartment where what seemed like strangers were standing around in the kitchen. Some of us went up to the roof to smoke and watch the city, throw the occasional beer bottle down onto a passerby below on the street.

After a while some of us went back downstairs to try to find Darby's friend. He was in his bedroom. The room was like the Blue House: dilapidated, with no furniture, just old photographs scotch-taped to the walls. He was sitting in a loose circle of people. I sat down and joined them.

It turned out he had been a model and the photos taped on the walls were of himself—before he became what he was now. There was old food on the carpeted floor, makeshift ashtrays and him, like a monk, sitting in the center of the tiny room.

He told us how he used to be beautiful, how he was a model in Paris and New York, how he worked for *French Vogue*, how one time he even met Warhol. He'd gesture as he told his story at photos on the walls as evidence of his previous life. In the photographs he was tan, muscular, handsome. Unrecognizable from the talking corpse before us. On the carpet, among the singe marks and small piles of food on paper plates and bits of garbage, was a paper crown with cotton glued on it. No one was looking, so I took it, folded it up and hid it in my jeans' back pocket.

A man walked in—without a shirt, wearing a mesh cap. He looked around the room as if he was trying to find something or someone, and then left. He could have been twenty or he could have been fifty. It was hard to tell.

Our friend, the corpse, got up and then so did Darby and then we all walked out. Everyone from the roof was coming down while me and Darby followed the corpse and his friends into a small, tight crowd of people, quickly moving into the kitchen.

There was a needle going around. I'd never seen one before but, for some reason, I wasn't scared though I knew I should've been. I looked up at the faces of the people standing in the circle. Not everyone had their sleeves rolled up but a few did. There were girls who looked like models. There were a couple other kids—they looked like they'd been living under an overpass—skinny with dirty hands and faces.

One of the model girls—with high cheekbones and huge brown eyes, her yellow hair pulled back—you could tell she had once been beautiful but now she was ruined. I recognized something in her posture, in her gaze— she had a desperation that was palpable. Like she'd given in completely, her entire being surrendered, a turning away from the world. She had her sleeve rolled up for something other than what the world was giving her. And in that moment, I was her—I didn't care what happened to me next. I wanted to feel the way she looked—ecstatic, resigned.

It is a dream that haunts me though I can never remember what it is. Its residue clings to me, a trace, like a hangover. It enters into me and I can't get rid of it because I don't have the words for what it is.

I can pick up radio frequencies from overseas. If it's in another language, I listen for the background noise. Once I heard gunfire, explosions in the distance.

chapter four

We slept on the floors of the burned-out cathedral. There were old rugs with blood on them, batteries and rusting metal parts. Piles of clothes, blankets and old stuffed animals. Burn holes in everything.

There were maybe eleven of us. Concrete floors and they were always cold.

The highway was in the distance. It took people away and at night I could hear the cars, like someone breathing heavy, but from far away. I'd lie awake wishing I were in one of those cars. Then I'd remember I didn't have anywhere to go.

Near the church there were these billboards for the highway. They were always changing but one I remember the most was an ad of a rich lady in a fur, sipping a diet cola from a straw. Next to it was another one of a skinny girl in a black cocktail dress eating French chocolate.

Between the two was where kids tossed their used syringes. You could get them at the pharmacy on Powell or Market. Or anyplace, really. You'd just tell the people in the pharmacy that you were diabetic and they had to give them to you.

The sun is as dangerous on cloudy days as it is on sunny days. Sunburn ointment is not designed to give complete protection against the excessive exposure. Sunbathing or dozing in the desert can be fatal.

Warning: one heat stroke is usually followed by others and is a warning that the entire group may be at risk. This is the "Weak Link Rule." The status of the whole group is assessed at this point.

Avoid all dogs and rats, which are the major carriers of fleas. Fleas are the primary carrier of plague and murine typhus.

Flies are abundant throughout desert environments. Filth-borne disease is a major health problem posed by flies. Dirt or insects in the desert can cause infection in minor cuts or scratches.

Mammals: dogs are often found near eating facilities and tend to travel in packs of eight or ten. Dogs are carriers of rabies and should be avoided. The leader must decide how to deal with packs of dogs; extermination and avoidance are two options. Dogs also carry fleas which may be transferred upon bodily contact. Rabies is present in most mammal populations. Do not take any chances of contracting fleas or rabies from any animal by adopting pets.

Burning is the best solution for waste.

One day me and Darby went shopping at the Salvation Army in Oakland. She bought this kids' t-shirt with an iron-on horse. I didn't find anything. I tried on a kids'-size pink ski suit but it ripped when I took it off.

We were shopping because it was Darby's birthday and we wanted to find something nice to wear. It was her seventeenth and we were going to this club called The MAB.

On our way home me and Darby ran into Talia. She was collecting old bottles and cans on Market. She had a garbage bag with her and she was slowly filling it up. She was trying to make enough money to buy some meth at the Tower. We stopped and offered her some of our soup-in-a-box.

Glanders:
Found naturally in horses, donkeys, and mules but humans can get it, too. Death rate is 100%.

O Fever
Small pox
Yellow Rain
Tularemia (rabbit or deer fever)

Nerve Agents:
Sarin
Soman
Tabun
VX
GF
Agent 15

Symptoms include: drool, dimmed or blurred vision. Involuntary urination and/or defecation. Blood-tinged saliva. Symptoms begin in seconds. Death can occur in 1-10 minutes.

Agent 15 symptoms include: dilated pupils, blurred vision, dry mouth, illusions, hallucinations, denial of illness, impaired memory and shortness of breath. When groups of people are affected, the group shares hallucinations.

Mass hysteria.

Me and Darby went up to the Tower to score some meth. There were these girls up there. They were almost dead. They were like animals that had been shot—they were twitching.

There were three of them with perfect skin and Hollywood teeth. But they had nothing with them and they were barely wearing anything. They looked like little kids.

I grabbed Darby by the wrist. "Come on, let's go," I said.

But, of course, we weren't going anywhere. Darby wanted to stay. We'd made a deal with this guy called LC: we could buy some really good meth for cheaper since we were buying more.

But I was scared about the girls. Their faces were blank and they were sniffling like kittens.

"Come on, Darby," I said, again. "Let's go."

But Darby wouldn't let me leave. She said if I left, LC would see it as a cop out and he'd come and find us. Plus, then we wouldn't get any meth from him. So I stayed.

Darby touched me on the arm then she went into the shut door under the stairs. I waited with the kitten-girls for Darby to come back.

The girls smelled like flowers and urine. I felt sick to my stomach. One of them came to life. She said, "Who are you?"

She was tall with long black hair. Her eyes were big. She stared at me, waiting. She couldn't seem to be able to keep her head up.

"Don't I know you?" she asked, really slow.

I didn't know her. And I wanted Darby to come back so I could leave.

"Is your name Treenie?" the girl asked, her black t-shirt slipping off her shoulder so I could see her skinny body, her flat chest.

I looked away, wishing Darby would return. Then the girl mumbled something and asked, "Don't I know you from home?"

I looked at her again. At her tiny white face and her green eyes and for a moment I thought maybe I did know her from someplace.

Darby came walking out the door and up to me. She didn't say anything. She just grabbed my elbow and steered me, walking really fast down the stairs and into the street below.

A month or so later the cops found that same girl's body in an abandoned car near the highway.

I heard that Napalm was locked-up again. But that this time the doctors dragged the world out of him. Left him empty, a ghost. Walking the hospital corridors, mumbling to himself. That the doctors had to keep putting him down to stop him from banging his head against the walls.

I saw him a few times after that. He was living in tent city near City Hall. I tried once to get him to talk to me but he wasn't Napalm anymore. It was like talking to someone who resembled Naplam, but wasn't him at all. He didn't say a word, he just looked at me like he had never seen me before. Finally he just turned and walked away.

I stare at the television, at the images of boys in black hooded sweatshirts and black jeans, military boots. Their faces covered in scarves, bandanas or black ski masks.

They run from the riot police who shoot tear gas into their faces. Some of the boys wear goggles to protect their eyes from the poison, some wear gas masks, others carry handkerchiefs doused in vinegar. The police drive large green trucks with twin water cannons mounted on top.

I stare at the image of the fenced-off coastal resort: the seven-mile-long barbed-wire fence where the protesters are kept outside, while inside world leaders meet to discuss finance, loans and interest rates. A sky of helicopters and fighter planes patrol the closed-off water and airspace.

I watch the boys, and how they run, their bodies filled with rage and desire.

I watch the boys, I close my eyes, and I try to will myself out of this room and to the place where they are running. I shut my eyes and I try to become one of them.

It's just a matter of time. Look at our cities with their modern office buildings and luxury hotels instead of housing for the poor. Cosmetic surgery clinics for the rich instead of hospitals. Families living in makeshift tents constructed of paper, clothing and blankets. Living off the garbage of the city.

The ghost of the television set: ads for skin cream to banish the lines on the face, pills to kill off the appetite. TV shows featuring emaciated women and ads selling endless pharmaceuticals. This is the language we are given. The language that takes the place of everything.

It is the language of commerce, the languge of numbers, of endless calculation.

But animals can't count. So they stay outside the system, a static, like the swarming of bees, that only they can hear.

He sleeps in the streets under skeletal desert-like bushes, on park benches, under freeway overpasses. On the concrete, along the sweet, toxic contaminants. And when the city shuts down at night, letting loose its phantoms, its dead engines, he wanders the streets looking for food in dumpsters, clothes or blankets. Mad Byzantine priest, Sweet and Lost Saint Francis. Scouring the city alleys for scraps of paper, matches, lighters, dog-eared books for scrawl. Only during the day, beneath the fever of the orange sky, does he sleep. And when he sleeps, he dreams of dogs.

1. don white headscarf with rising sun motif.
2. wind around waist the belt of a thousand stitches, crafted by a thousand women making one stitch each.
3. drink a cup of sake.
4. compose and recite death poem—traditional for samurai prior to hari-kari.

When I call, the operator answers. She wants to know if I need any help. I don't know if she means help with the phone call or help with my life. I hang up when she asks again.

I stand in the phone booth with my hand on the telephone trying to light a cigarette. I don't know where I am or what I am doing. I forget everything—erased, like an un-done tape.

Then I remember: Toby is out there somewhere and I have to find him.

chapter five

"Come on Darby, get up."

Darby had been sleeping, I swear, nonstop since we left LA. She'd moved from the back seat to the front, but other than that, she was luggage.

"Come on, get up."

We'd driven from Santa Cruz down to LA and then out into the desert. Darby had somehow managed to talk to someone who talked to someone who lent her their silver Camaro. I assumed she'd be owing a magnificent favor when we returned but I didn't ask.

We'd been through Barstow, Bakers, and every little methed-out, Born Again town in between. I'd told Darby I'd wake her when we reached Reno and here we were, parked under the glittering red-and-white lights of the pawnshop marquees. We'd driven this far to buy a gun. We'd done what we could back home to get a car. Now we were finally doing it.

Darby was up now, scratching her head.

"What the fuck?" she asked, coughing, lighting up her first cigarette of the morning. Running her fingers through her long black hair, Darby had made her way out of the car to sit on the sidewalk.

"Give me one of those," I said, reaching for her good cigarettes. "Where have you been hiding them anyway?"

Darby handed me a Marlboro Red and tossed me her unicorn lighter.

"There you go," she said, as she took out a second cigarette and lit that one, too.

We both sat there on the curb, the heat coming off the concrete. It must have been eight or nine in the morning but the bars were open already, had been open all night, the smell of beer and urine in the air.

"Where are they?" Darby asked quietly.

I smoked my cigarette, looking away.

I didn't want to answer so I kept smoking, looking off into the distance like I was looking at something or thinking of something profound. Before she asked again, I got up and walked back to the car.

The doors were open and I climbed in the back to the heap of clothes, all dirty, and grabbed a t-shirt. It smelled so I threw it back in the pile, deciding to keep on the one I'd been wearing for the past week. It was a pajama top from when I was little. Made of cotton with tiny brown tigers on it, just their faces. When we left, I cut the arms off so now the t-shirt was a tank top of sorts.

Darby called my name, about to ask, again.

But I didn't want to talk, so I got up, lit another cigarette, and walked away.

I hadn't eaten since we left LA. I hadn't eaten since I don't know when. I was wearing my old Wranglers and they were starting to fall off me. I couldn't make another hole in my belt. I'd run out of belt. I'd been living off warm Cola and cigarettes. My body, disintegrating.

"Hey, what's up?" Darby was back at me, again.

"They live in the hills," I said. "They're poor and they live in the hills," I mumbled, then I crawled over the car's stick shift, over to the driver's seat, turned the key in the ignition and pressed the button on the dash that turned the music on.

"Candy," Darby yelled. "He's opening up the shop."

Darby was still sitting on the curb, smoking. But now she was pointing her smoking hand at the man pushing the bars open to his shop.

The last time I'd seen my brother, even though he was four years older than me, he was so skinny he looked like a girl.

He was sitting under the bridge near the river. He called me over. "Candy," he said, "come over here."

I went over to him, even though I knew what he wanted to say would be bad.

"Candy, come here."

He was wearing dark glasses. Toward the end, he always wore dark glasses. I didn't know if it was because he was using so much by that point or if he just wore them as protection against the world.

His face was white like a moon.

"Look, I know I've been a shit for a brother."

His voice was small and breaking, his words, starting to slur. It scared me to see him like that. I'd seen him bad before but that last night was the worst.

In his hand was his silver cross and charms. He'd worn some of them on a necklace around his neck but he'd stopped when he realized someone might take them from him when he got sick. The charms were of the places he wanted to go and then one was of a rabbit. The necklace and charms weren't technically worth anything. He'd been carrying them with him for good luck. He put his hand in my hand, dripping the necklace. I knew what it meant for him to give me the necklace so I tried to get him to take it back but he wouldn't. After some time I gave up and I let him put the necklace around my neck.

"Don't take it off," he said. "Promise."

I couldn't stay any longer because I knew if I did, I would start crying and I knew I needed to be strong so he would maybe not give up.

After that I never saw my brother again.

"Let's go in," Darby said, grabbing my arm.

I was still in the front of the car so Darby dragged me out the front seat, laughing.

"Come on," she said, "let's get this over with."

We had to ring the bell to get in. Once the man saw us, he walked behind the counter and reached under to let us in. The door opened then it slammed and locked behind us.

The room was filled with stuff everywhere: jewelry in glass cases, cameras and televisions stacked in piles. There were stranger things, too, like what looked like diamond tiaras and costumes for the circus or girls on the strip.

Along the wall was a mounted deer head and in a glass cabinet nearby were two stuffed baby deer. One was curled up as if it was sleeping and the other, in flight, its tiny brown feet in the air.

Darby nudged me and whispered, "Look."

I followed her gaze to a locked glass case behind the counter. Inside were piles of guns: tiny pistols, police handguns and hunting rifles.

"How much is that?" Darby asked, pointing to a blue pearl pistol in the case.

It was beautiful. The grip was blurred royal blue and then the machinery of the pistol was black but it was a factory-like black, matte, about the size of my hand.

The man said nothing, smiling. He walked over to the case and opened it. He took the pistol out and gave it to Darby.

Darby handed the pistol to me. It was heavier than I imagined and it made my arm drop. The man walked over to me and helped me hold it, taking my hand in his.

"You hold the pistol with one hand, generally speaking. But it's okay if you need both to position it to shoot. Here you are," he said, placing my fingers on the gun. "It's a small one. I'm sure you can manage it," he said as he walked away.

I'd never held one before. I had always imagined aiming and shooting would be like drawing through air. The weight had never occurred to me.

"Which one of you is the boy?" the man asked, laughing, lighting a cigarette.

 I set the gun down on the glass case then I reached for the back of my neck. I took my brother's necklace off, closed the clasp and set it down. "What's this worth?" I ask.

The man looked at me then he looked at the necklace. Then he looked at me again. "Not much," he said. "Got anything else?"

Darby moved up and started untying her boots. "You can take these," she said.

"Darby," I said, but she stops me.

"I don't need them."

Darby tried to sell her boots to the man but I wouldn't let her. When she got bored, she went next door to see if she could get some beer at the bar. I stayed behind, told Darby I was going to try to get the man to lower the price of the gun.

After Darby cleared out and some time passed so I knew she was charming her way to a few free beers, I talked to the man.

He wanted the ring Toby had given me. It was worthless but I loved it because it was all I had left of him. It was a metal band with his initial's carved in it and the words, "Honesty is its own defense," carved inside.

The man saw the ring and he wanted it because he knew it meant something to me.

"You can't have that," I said. "It doesn't belong to me."

Then I put my hand on his arm.

chapter six

Five days lost.

Black ribbons in my hair.

Darby's holding a blue pearl pistol. The car's got no AC. The windows are rolled all the way down and dirt and dust are on my face. Like ceremonial ritual—me and Darby and a gun, lost in the desert, swallowing these mouthfuls of the past.

We've been on a diet of mini lemon pies we bought five for a dollar at the Dollar Thrift. That and warm beer.

Pull over somewhere in the Biblical desert.

My arms and hands trembling, I open the car door and throw-up white foam.

Dizzy, I look up at the blackening sky. Mica velvet, it looks like molten lava, and rumbles past.

Nothing but death and tumbleweed, nothing but barbed wire and fallout.

Toxic jackrabbits and dead coyotes on the side of the road.

At the last Conoco station I filled the tank and made my way to the toilet.

My hair looks like a wig from days without wash and the dry heat of the sun.

Darby's still sleeping so I rifle through her things and find a small container of blue cream eye shadow in her pink plastic ballerina case. I brought it with me into the bathroom.

After smoking for I don't know how long, having ripped the filter tips off, I dip my pinkie in the tiny plastic make-up container and trace a stream of Darby's blue magnetic eye shadow onto my lids. Confused, I stare in the mirror for a while, then I draw a trace of blue onto my cheeks. War paint.

When I got back to the car, the metal was humming from the heat and Darby was still in the back seat of the car sleeping, her arms around her small body.

Driving ninety on the highway listening to old Fugazi.

My mouth is open like I'm screaming but no sound comes out.

Standing in the empty lot of a Sinclair filling station in the middle of the high desert. I'm standing inside the glass box of the pay phone.

I'm standing in the lot of the filling station in the brutal white film of the desert.

I bought another case of cheap beer, washed my hair in the bathroom sink, stood under the flickering white lights of the station's marquee. After a while, I made my way to the phone booth.

"I can't take it anymore, Toby," I say into the telephone receiver in my hand. "I can't."

But Toby isn't on the other line. No one is on the other line because Toby isn't there. Because no one is ever there when I call his number. It just rings and rings.

I'm standing in the telephone booth in the middle of the desert, smoking cigarette after cigarette, the sky the only thing moving, my hands shaking.

I wake dreaming on my knees, again.

On the side of the highway, I am kneeling when I wake from a dream of the ranch and the horses and my brother, who is still alive.

He helps me get up so I can sit on the back of Princess, my childhood pony. He gets on his horse and I follow him, the two of us racing across the yellow sage into the mountains.

Someone is calling my name. But when I turn my head to look, I see nothing. Nothing but scrub and dust and the black sky moving her magnetics over me.

The man comes to me so I know I must be dreaming, again. He is tall and thin and wearing a simple black suit, black work boots. His hair is long, to his ears, and the color of black night. I always see him from far away—and he makes his way toward me: his long body moving slowly. He has a limp and he uses a walking cane. When he finally comes up to me, he takes my face in his hands. I wake when his lips begin to mouth my name.

chapter seven

I wake on the pale pink plush of a hotel room. Burn marks on my arms, the glittering cream of baby-blue eyeshadow smeared on my arms and my legs. Blood or lipstick, its rich red crimson, stained on my fingers and hands. The smell of old beer on my skin. I don't know whose hotel room I am in, I don't know what hotel or what city. What time of day. I don't know my own name. My mind, emptied out.

The telephone is ringing. But I don't know where from. It takes what feels like a lifetime to make my way across the floor. I'm crawling on my bare hands and knees and make my way to the telephone. I reach to pick up the receiver but just as I do, the ringing stops.

Then a knocking on the door. I can't lift my body from the floor so I wait in terror. After a while, the knocking stops.

The room I am in is immense. A suite, I imagine, a penthouse. The room is vast and long and empty with enormous glass windows. I can't move, my body is frozen, like my mind. Stuck in something that happened, something terrible, that I can't, no matter how hard I try, remember. I don't know how I got here or where I am. What city. Whose room. How many days or weeks or months I've lost. From the center of the vast room, I can see a city: enormous but silent, muted from the threshold of the windows.

I remember the desert and driving and I remember a motel room and then everything goes blank. I was trying to find Toby. I kept trying to call him from filling station payphones. Something happened.

I think that I saw him: Toby, his voice and his face, criminal, beautiful. And then I remember: I didn't see him, it was only a dream.

I sit on the huge bed in the middle of the dark hotel room eating bright candy I found in the pockets of my coat. Small mouthfuls—one gummy bear at a time. Vodka and chocolate pudding I order from room service.

I call and call the number I have for Toby. No one ever answers. I sit on the cold tile floor of the bathroom holding the receiver, listening to its rings.

"Toby," I say, "I don't know where you are. I'm here, Toby, I'm waiting."

The pain is excruciating, it's beautiful. Redefining me, creating new limits. Like a sharp metal knife. I sit on the hotel room floor counting the hours.

I'm awake or else I'm dreaming. There's a knock on the door.

When we were little my mother would make costumes for us: me, my little sister, and my brother. Every Halloween, she'd make us hand-sewn cat costumes. She made white gloves from cotton for the cat paws, drawing claws with a black Sharpie pen. Painting four black lines for each paw. Black eyeliner for our eyes, making us feline. Whiskers on our face and a tiny triangle for a nose. She'd walk us door to door, holding the plastic orange pumpkin for us as it filled with candy.

After Halloween, I'd wear my costume for months until the cotton wore thin. To bed and around the yard, imagining I was a wild animal, conjuring an imaginary world in which I might live. Behind the mask is another mask, my grandfather used to say, referring to the cops, their uniforms and hats, how they'd hide behind their authority. Anonymous criminals, he'd say.

I wanted something else. I didn't want to be like that though. Wearing the costume was like disappearing into the background, a wallflower, as my history teacher used to call me. Here, but gone. I liked wearing the costume my mother made me because wearing it made me feel like I had a key to another, alternative world. That when I wore it I could step out of this one and into the next.

I don't eat anymore. Just mouthfuls of candy and glasses of vodka. One gummy bear, one glass of vodka. One sour ball, one glass of vodka. One spoonful of warm chocolate pudding, one tall glass of vodka.

I move my body in slow motion across the room, stare into the long mirror.

I don't sleep. I just sit on the shag floor of the hotel room and wait.

I wake on the floor to the smell of fire. I can't get up. After a while, I lift myself up and make my way, slowly, to the bathroom.

There is a fire in the sink: red flames and small bits of ash floating above a flame. I don't know where the fire is coming from. When I walk out of the bathroom and back into the bedroom, I notice all the windows are open. Then I look at my own body: I'm nude and there's a small cut in my left wrist. It's new.

The room is in disarray: books and magazines on the floor, wrappers from candy, a series of makeshift ashtrays spilling over in ash, old cigarette butts. Empty glasses on the tables and the floor. I walk over to the bureau and drink warm vodka from a teacup. It tastes sharp like swallowing small shards of glass. Then I light up a cigarette and sit back down on the soft shag.

When my parents left my brother and I behind I don't remember saying goodbye or their returning. I don't remember anything.

After what feels like weeks in the hotel room, I call the front desk and ask whose room I am in. The man at the front desk pauses when I ask. He tells me the room is under my name. When I ask who paid for the room, he puts me on hold and never returns.

Later that afternoon when I try to get up, lift my body in an attempt to leave the room, maybe go down to the bar, my body falls limp and I drop to the floor.

When I wake some time later, my legs are bruised already, small blue splotches on my thighs.

I am coating my face in the clear, wet emollient of the past.

Here, where I am, the taper candles never go out.
I cover my body in its invisible light.
And the dead enter the way music enters the minds of the sick.

Escape was impossible and everyone I knew then is gone now, dead, or else in prison.

Their names, like glass jars lined along the corridors.
The murmuring ceremonies of memory.

I touch the wound and I begin to speak.

At night in the dark hotel room, I sit inside the terror.

When the darkness arrives it threatens to destroy me. I ask someone who I don't know, someone invisible, someone who must be listening to me, *Please, guide me.* I ask, "What will I do with this body, the terrible ruin of this mind?" I ask and ask, in a language I don't recognize.

But they never answer. Or, if they do, I never hear them.

I sit for hours, for days, on the floor of the hotel room waiting for the call, the knock on the door, waiting for Toby's arrival.

Toby, where are you?

I sit on the floor in the darkness, not eating, not sleeping, waiting for his call.

Toby, can you hear me?

I sit on the floor in the hotel room, listening to the darkness under the water of the silence.

My body is cold when I touch it, from too much drink and smoking and not eating.

"I'm going to die in here," I say, to no one.

I wake in the large white bed, my arms around Sparkle, my tiny Steiff, a gift from a man whose name I never knew. I wake with this little dead thing, this object of immense beauty and sorrow, in my arms.

Toby, can you hear me? I'm coming to the end now.

chapter eight

Toby, thinner than ever, dancing jagged, in ripped black jeans with zippers up the crotch. From who knows where. His body too small now, the jeans slowly slipping off.

Toby, alone, dancing to his own silent music. Leather cuffs on his wrists, new blue tattoos on the pale insides of his arms.

Toby, slipping into some delicate spell of heroin or who knows what. Moving, always moving.

Toby, gone already. Toby now just the trace of Toby, the delicate spell of the dream.

I wear a blonde bobbed wig and carry a silver switchblade with me everywhere.

I asked Germ to shave my head. I told him I want to be free of everything holding me back.

Static and noise inside my head like a radio station spinning between dials.

This is what they said it would be like.

During the night I wander the city streets. I don't eat, so I am a ghost.
I wear children's clothes. An old t-shirt with an iron-on pink pony and
boy's Rustler jeans.

Candy, they say, *Candy*, when I walk by. The highway, the ocean,
the tiny brown and gray birds hidden inside the universe of the tree.
Candy, they say, *Candy*.

Moving through the streets in a deep sleep as if maybe one day
something will happen, something entirely new will appear out of
nowhere and then finally everything will change.

Then, at last, my life will begin.

I have this fake halo and stars on my arms.

Cat eyes with black liner. White face powder to ward off the elements.

After what happened, I don't talk to anyone.

Garbage, waste, sewage. I was born one chromosome short of genius, one chromosome short of idiot. I was born on a US military base, in the age of infinite calculation, of glittering markets and the magic of endless repetition.

Toby wakes in parked cars, his head against the glass. Under a willow, under an overpass. Always more men, so many and he can never remember.

When he was small, Casey, his hound dog was his best friend.

His childhood is old rusting cars in the yard, sleepy horses near the shed. And always, in the pines, an invisible cacophony of birds.

His childhood is a craft moving along the water, its searchlights coming closer but never, never reaching him.

Someone pulls out a plastic bag, the little kind you get when you buy a handful of penny candy from the corner store. Toby does it first. He takes a big huff from the bag. His eyes get wet, his face changes. Then he drops to the ground.

No one saw Darby again but someone said she was back in town. That she was climbing into cars with men she didn't know for money.

She'd stay in crack houses like she was dead already, nodding off to her own distant thrumming. Doing impossible favors for a hit.

On Mission Street, on the road leading to the ramp out to the highway, Toby stands in the middle of two streams of traffic. His body, so thin now he looks like a twelve-year-old. But his face is the face of an old man.

He's wearing a pair of worn-out jeans and black leather boots, a trucker's hat with the word *Preacher* on the front. His t-shirt too big for him now, it hangs from his body.

He stands in the middle of traffic, walking up to each car window, asking for money. People roll up their windows when they see him, lock their car doors.

A woman in a Volvo slows down when she pulls up to where Toby is standing. She's tan with blonde, highlighted hair, wearing a pair of aviator glasses. Toby's face is dark with poverty tan and there are bits of dried something on his face: old food or skin coming off from too much meth.

When he walks up to her car window, she reaches over to the console and grabs some quarters from her toll collection. She doesn't look at him as she puts the money in his hand. As soon as he takes the money, she presses the button that rolls the window back up and locks her car doors.

I woke up in Children's Hospital. Alone, in a bed.

When I heard that Toby was dead I checked myself into a hotel with the money some man had given me. I did the last of the heroin, eager to enter that soft warm coma.

Clusterfuck of television. Teenage slumland. Little Toby lost in the middle of a dream: NASCAR, dumpster, car lot landscape. Turning mean on the streets, kneeling into rooms, doing anything for love or for money—

In the backseat of the crimson Mercedes sedan.

Cottonwood, milkweed. The taste of cold metal.
The repetition of 3 AM sirening ambulance rides.

Yellow cream, three-tiered birthday cake. Cherry lip balm. Pale blue satin shorts and matching jacket with my name embroidered in hot pink.

Poochie, my childhood beagle, whimpering inside the locked rooms of night.

A field of black-and-white dappled ponies. Blinding, the silence.

An orange plastic lighter, and red gas-station canister of kerosene.

I got a halo on my head and these animal fangs. Beige-blonde hair cut short to a boy's haircut. In my t-shirts and pjs, I'm a silent princess, a light warrior, a small song no one will ever hear.

You ask why I starve myself, why all my friends are dead.

ACKNOWLEDGEMENTS

The title of this book comes from a Fugazi album of the same name.

Grateful acknowledgment is made to the following journals in which chapters from this book first appeared:

Bennington Review
Schlag Magazine

Cynthia Cruz is the author of seven collections of poems including *Hotel Oblivion*, which won the National Book Critics Circle Award and was a finalist for the Kingsley Tufts Award. She is also the author of *Disquieting: Essays on Silence*, a collection of essays exploring silence as a form of resistance, and *The Melancholia of Class: A Manifesto for the Working Class*, a book about Freudian melancholia and the working class. She is the recipient of fellowships from Yaddo, MacDowell and Princeton University's Hodder Fellowship. She lives in Berlin, Germany.

PUBLICATION OF THIS BOOK WAS MADE POSSIBLE
BY GRANTS AND DONATIONS. WE ARE ALSO GRATEFUL
TO THOSE INDIVIDUALS WHO PARTICIPATED IN
OUR BUILD A BOOK PROGRAM. THEY ARE:

Anonymous (14), Robert Abrams, Michael Ansara, Kathy Aponick,
Jean Ball, Sally Ball, Clayre Benzadon, Adrian Blevins, Laurel Blossom,
Adam Bohannon, Betsy Bonner, Patricia Bottomley, Lee Briccetti,
Joel Brouwer, Susan Buttenwieser, Anthony Cappo, Paul and Brandy
Carlson, Dan Clarke, Mark Conway, Elinor Cramer, Kwame Dawes,
Michael Anna de Armas, John Del Peschio, Brian Komei Dempster,
Rosalynde Vas Dias, Patrick Donnelly, Lynn Emanuel, Blas Falconer,
Jennifer Franklin, John Gallaher, Reginald Gibbons, Rebecca Kaiser
Gibson, Dorothy Tapper Goldman, Julia Guez, Naomi Guttman and
Jonathan Mead, Forrest Hamer, Luke Hankins, Yona Harvey, KT Herr,
Karen Hildebrand, Carlie Hoffman, Glenna Horton, Thomas and
Autumn Howard, Catherine Hoyser, Elizabeth Jackson, Linda Susan
Jackson, Jessica Jacobs and Nickole Brown, Lee Jenkins, Elizabeth
Kanell, Nancy Kassell, Maeve Kinkead, Victoria Korth, Brett Lauer
and Gretchen Scott, Howard Levy, Owen Lewis and Susan Ennis,
Margaree Little, Sara London and Dean Albarelli, Tariq Luthun, Myra
Malkin, Louise Mathias, Victoria McCoy, Lupe Mendez, Michael and
Nancy Murphy, Kimberly Nunes, Susan Okie and Walter Weiss, Cathy
McArthur Palermo, Veronica Patterson, Jill Pearlman, Marcia and
Chris Pelletiere, Sam Perkins, Susan Peters and Morgan Driscoll, Maya
Pindyck, Megan Pinto, Kevin Prufer, Martha Rhodes and Jean Brunel,
Paula Rhodes, Louise Riemer, Peter and Jill Schireson, Rob Schlegel,
Yoana Setzer, Soraya Shalforoosh, Mary Slechta, Diane Souvaine,
Barbara Spark, Catherine Stearns, Jacob Strautmann, Yerra Sugarman,
Arthur Sze and Carol Moldaw, Marjorie and Lew Tesser, Dorothy
Thomas, Rushi Vyas, Martha Webster and Robert Fuentes, Rachel
Weintraub and Allston James, Abby Wender and Rohan Weerasinghe,
and Monica Youn.